RIDDLE ROAD

Also by Elizabeth Spires and Erik Blegvad

WITH ONE WHITE WING: PUZZLES IN POEMS AND PICTURES

Margaret K. McElderry Books

ELIZABETH SPIRES

RIDDLE ROAD

PUZZLES IN POEMS AND PICTURES

ILLUSTRATED BY ERIK BLEGVAD

MARGARET K. MCELDERRY BOOKS

"Three sat down at the table" was first published as "Riddle" in *Food Fight*,
edited by Michael J. Rosen, published by Harcourt Brace & Company.

Margaret K. McElderry Books
An imprint of Simon & Schuster Children's Publishing Division
1230 Avenue of the Americas
New York, New York 10020

Book design by Michael Nelson
The text of this book is set in Baskerville.
The illustrations are rendered in watercolor.

Printed in Hong Kong
First Edition
10 9 8 7 6 5 4 3 2

Library of Congress Cataloging-in-Publication Data
Spires, Elizabeth.
Riddle road: puzzles in poems and pictures / Elizabeth Spires;
illustrated by Erik Blegvad.—1st ed.
p. cm.
Summary: A collection of twenty-six original riddles
with clues given in the illustrations.
ISBN 0-689-81783-5
1. Children's poetry. 2. Puzzles—Juvenile literature. 3. Riddles, Juvenile.
[1. Riddles. 2. Picture Puzzles.]
I. Blegvad, Erik, ill. II. Title.
PN6109.97S667 1999
97-36592

For Bill and Alice

—E. S.

For Kaye, Esmé, Viggo, and Harald Noah

—E. B.

When one doesn't know what it is, then it is something;
but when one knows what it is, then it is nothing.

—Old Swedish Riddle

North, south,
east, west,
we run along
and never rest.

Where are we going?
Everywhere!
We never stop
until we're there.

roads

People hate me,
people depend on me.
It's alarming
how loud I can be!

alarm clock

It's curious
how curious
I am.

I eyeball everything.
I am what I
sound like.

I am, I am, I am!

eye

Have you ever seen a horse
swimming in the sea?
A horse without a rider,
splashing gracefully?

A horse so small
it would fit in your hand?
A horse you'll never find
galloping on the land?

seahorse

I live in a glass house.
I only fear ice.
I should be worth a lot
but I'm not.

goldfish

Two of us, there's always two.
One won't do.
We look like each other.
We do.

We've been everywhere
you've been.
We're a pair
you can't do without.

shoes

I have a tongue but no mouth.
Still, loud or soft,
I can sound off.
Good news or bad,
glad tidings or sad,
it's the same to me.
Name me! Name me!

bell

We listen to wishes
but have no ears.

We're at home in the dark
without any fears.

We're older than you
by millions of years.

When you're gone forever,
we'll still be here.

Near or far,
can you guess what we are?

stars

For years you have us all,
then, one by one, we fall.
No matter what you do, you lose us.
Even if you keep us, you lose us.

Reinforcements arrive,
more white coats like us,
who won't be pushed around,
who mean to stand their ground!

baby teeth

My pedals will get you nowhere.
My keys open no locks.
Sometimes I stand upright.
Sometimes I'm a big baby on all fours.

Sit down and play
and you'll have a grand time.

piano

Needles and pins,
needles and pins,
my nightmares are full
of needles and pins.

Ouch! Ouch!
And ouch again!
Please don't stick me
with needles and pins.

pincushion

A long time ago
I set out on a journey.
I crept from there to here.

I took what I could pack
and carry on my back.
Maybe I'll get there next year.

snail

I eat words wherever
I find them but am no wiser.
Keep your books under lock and key
or they'll be devoured by me!

bookworm

I hang out at ball games,
on street corners, and at barbecues.
My bite is worse than my bark.
I'm a dog you'll never walk on a leash.

hot dog

Three sat down at the table.
Two worked together while the third watched.
There was a stabbing, a robbery, and a cut throat.
When the maid walked in, the third jumped in the soup.
Taken away, they were found not guilty.
Tomorrow, they'll be at it again.

knife, fork, and spoon

Have you ever watched a lighthouse
flashing in the dark?

Have you ever seen a flashlight
turning on and off?

Now think of something smaller
that blinks from dusk to dawn.

There I am! Catch me.
Catch me if you can.

firefly

I'm stripped to the bone
and live alone
in the closet.

I have a head, arms, legs,
but no hat, no clothes,
no shoes.

Despite it all,
I always
smile.

You'd think I'd complain,
but I make no bones
about it.

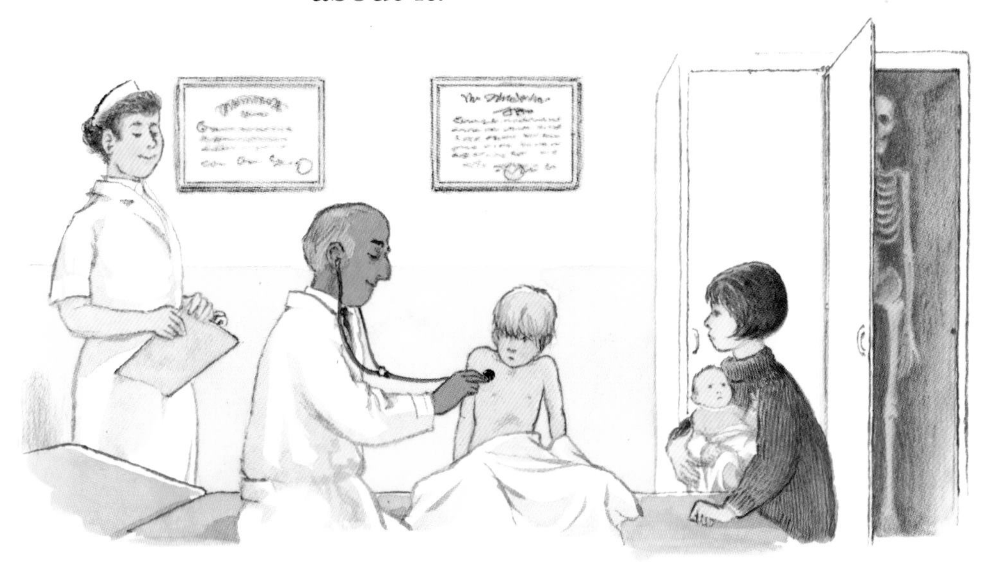

skeleton

A king met a king,
a queen a queen.
They stared and glared
and declared war
as, one by one,
their court disappeared.

chess

Stop telling me
my house is on fire,
my children are gone!

Is that any way
to treat a lady?
I'll fly away! I will!

ladybug

First I'm hungry, very hungry.
Then I'm sleepy, very sleepy.
I wrap myself up for a nap
and dream I have wings
and a coat of many colors.
When I wake up, I'll fly
in circles around you!

caterpillar

I look different
in order to look the same.
If stones move and trees see,
it is my doing.
Tell me my name.

chameleon

Have you ever felt the heat? I have.
Have you ever been steamed up? I have.
Have you ever wanted to sing? I have.
Have you ever screamed your head off? I have!

teakettle

I'm white as milk, but I'm not milk.
I'm fine as salt, but I'm not salt.
I'm sweet as honey, but I'm not honey.

A pinch, a spoonful, a pound,
A little or a lot, I come in any size.
Taste me, and you'll know what I am.

sugar

Once, I lived in the forest.
I was kidnapped by a man with an ax,
really a nice old man.

Now stars hang on my arms
and my hair is filled with light.
I can't wait for tonight.

Christmas tree

Dreams live inside me,
but don't open me.
If you do, they'll
vanish in thin air,
feathers flying everywhere!

pillow

I can be new or old.
I can be thin or full.
I can be big or small.
I can be bright or dull.
Like change in your pocket,
I'm different each night.

moon